SPECIMEN ZERO

Laura Shenton

SPECIMEN ZERO

Laura Shenton

Iridescent Toad Publishing

Iridescent Toad Publishing.

Cover by ZoneArtz Design.

First edition. ISBN: 978-1-913779-67-2

Prologue

D r Arthur Fleming's office was a testament to his dedication, or perhaps obsession, with his work. Papers, journals and textbooks lay strewn across every surface, creating an imposing labyrinth of knowledge that seemed to mirror the complexities of his mind. The dimly lit room was cast in long shadows from the towering bookshelves, imbuing it with an air of mystery.

"Another day, another rejection," he complained bitterly.

He crumpled up the letter he had just received and threw it in the wastepaper basket by his desk to join countless others, each one a reminder of his struggle for recognition within the scientific community. He slumped back in his chair, running a hand through his thinning hair as he stared blankly at the ceiling.

It taunted him to think that maybe they were right. Deep down though, despite everything he had achieved so far, he yearned for more. Convinced that he was smarter than his colleagues, he found it maddening to see lesser minds receive praise while his own ideas went unnoticed.

He raised a hand to his brow as his eyes scanned the shelves before him. He had spent years working on numerous projects, poring over countless research papers and devoting every spare second to his work. Yet, despite his unwavering dedication, to him, his career was at a stalemate.

"Damn it all," he muttered under his breath as he clenched his fists.

As he glanced around the small, stuffy room, he observed the stacks of books and papers that cluttered the surfaces. Some were dog-eared from frequent use, while others had been discarded after a single read. In his mind, there was no time to waste on ideas that were anything short of revolutionary.

Anxious to find some reassurance somehow, he told himself that perhaps he was simply ahead of his time. The notion brought him little comfort as he felt the familiar sting of inadequacy gnawing at the edges of his consciousness. It was a feeling he had known since his youth – one that had driven him to excel academically and pursue a career at the forefront of scientific research.

As the years had worn on, with his hair greying and with his face more lined, he felt the burden of his solitude weighing heavily upon him. It was a constant reminder that, despite his desire to be exceptional, he was prone to the same weaknesses and frailties as everyone else.

The other aspects of his life had long since crumbled around him. Despite his many accomplishments, he had never managed to find lasting happiness in his personal life. His relationships were always short-lived, with most women unable to tolerate his obsession with his work and the resulting emotional distance. Without approval – and ideally, praise – from his peers, there was little else to give him the sense of satisfaction that he so desperately craved.

Approaching what could only be described as a mid-life crisis, he had committed himself to his work with renewed fervour, seeking solace in the one thing that had never let him down: science.

Prepared to face yet another day in his never-ending quest for validation, with a heavy sigh, Dr Fleming grabbed one of the many pens strewn across his desk and began to write a list of ideas for potential proposal. Little did he know that the seeds of an idea were already beginning to take root deep within his brilliant but tortured mind.

Chapter One

Dr Arthur Fleming stood before the specimen in the laboratory, his eyes gleaming with excitement as he revelled in his efforts. The pristine white lab coat he wore failed to hide his scruffy casual clothes that he hadn't changed for days. As he contemplated the sight before him, his fingers absently tapped a pen against his clipboard, creating a rhythmic sound that echoed throughout the room.

Inside a tightly sealed glass beaker, was the alien he had labelled Specimen Zero. The creature's slender green body betrayed ethereal patterns that resembled an intricate constellation.

Dr Fleming gestured grandly at the display.

"I have every confidence in this, Dr Carver," he

announced. "My findings on Specimen Zero's spirituality will be nothing short of revolutionary."

Dr Amelia Carver leaned forward, her brow furrowed with concern as she took in the sight before her. She couldn't deny the brilliance of the opportunity to study such a being, but something about it gnawed at her conscience.

She hesitated, keen to choose her words carefully.

"Although the data will certainly be fascinating, I can't help but feel uneasy about the methods we're using to obtain it."

"Uneasy?" Dr Fleming scoffed, his arrogance shining through. "This will be groundbreaking research, Dr Carver! We're going to unlock the secrets of an entirely new form of spirituality – one that could change the course of human history."

He turned back to the captive alien, admiring the being like a piece of fine art.

"I understand," Dr Carver said cautiously. "I'm just concerned for the wellbeing of Specimen Zero. It's clear that our tests so far have caused it distress."

She glanced over at the alien. With its scope for movement restricted in its glass enclosure, its once vibrant body now drooped listlessly, and its gentle, expressive eyes seemed clouded with sadness.

Dr Fleming let out a snort and dismissed his colleague's concerns with a wave of his hand.

"Any distress on the subject is merely an unfortunate by-product of our research," he said. "It's a small price to pay for the sake of scientific advancement. Besides, it's an alien. It doesn't feel pain the way we do."

"Perhaps not," Dr Carver conceded. "But it's sentient, and clearly intelligent. We have a responsibility to treat it with compassion."

She took a step closer to the enclosure, her heart aching for the captive creature.

"Compassion?" Dr Fleming mocked, his face twisting into a sneer. "That's exactly the kind of sentimental nonsense that holds science back. This is not a pet. It's an invaluable test subject in our research."

Dr Carver watched as Specimen Zero pressed a clawed hand against the glass in longing for freedom. She couldn't help but wonder if they were the ones who needed to learn compassion from the alien. Despite its captivity, there was a resilience in its eyes, a strength derived from a hope and faith that their research had yet to quantify, or perhaps even acknowledge.

"Dr Fleming," she said softly, her voice laced with determination. "We need to find another way – a way that doesn't involve causing distress to Specimen Zero."

Dr Fleming merely shook his head, unable to comprehend Dr Carver's point of view.

"You're being naive, Dr Carver. But I suppose I shouldn't expect any less. You're young and idealistic," he said dismissively. "We can't afford to let sentimentality stand in our way. My work on Specimen Zero will change everything we know about spirituality and consciousness."

Dr Carver dug her nails into her palms, fighting to keep her composure as she watched Dr Fleming return to his research with a cold, detached air. The hum of machinery filled the room, punctuating the tense silence that went on to settle between them.

Chapter Two

The world outside the glass beaker was a mystery to Ke. He could see it, but he couldn't touch it or feel it. He was trapped, confined to an existence that wasn't his own. The wall of his prison was smooth and cold, and he could feel the weight of it all around him.

He was alone in there, with only his thoughts for company. He knew that he was there against his will, but he couldn't remember how he had ended up there. He could remember his old home, the warm sun on his back and the soft grass under his feet. But now, all he could see was the sterile metallic walls of the lab.

As he looked around, his heart pounded in his chest. There was nowhere to run, and nowhere to hide. He felt like a tiny insect under a microscope, being studied and stared at by beings who seemed to think themselves better than him.

The glass beaker gave Ke little choice but to sit in a hunched position. As the fluorescent lights above reflected off his smooth lime-green skin, his rib cage was clearly visible, each bone pressing against the surface of his body like a series of ominous notes on a xylophone. The muscles that enveloped his frame gave him an appearance of lean strength, yet there was a sense of vulnerability to him as well.

His head was crowned with a scythe-shaped point, giving him an otherworldly and menacing look. Substantially more prominent than his tiny ears, his teeth – a row of sharp points that gleamed like daggers under the sterile lighting – dominated his face. Although his eyes were small, they were no less expressive than any human's. The pupils within the long, slanted eyelids conveyed an intense intelligence and emotional depth.

His very soul full with sadness and indignation, he didn't want to be here, trapped in this laboratory like some animal. He wished to return home more than anything, but he knew that attempting to escape would most likely require him to cause harm to others. A peaceful creature with a kind and sensitive nature, he couldn't bear the thought of causing suffering.

He glanced down at his hands, which resembled elongated digits with claw-like nails. They were capable of great destruction. His feet, not unlike smooth, green bear paws, seemed out of place on his otherwise lithe body.

Ke closed his eyes and focused on the space between himself and his captors. He was so near, and yet so far, from the very people who he could only assume had been complicit in having taken so much from him.

Lost and disorientated, the monotony of his existence weighed heavily on him. He felt as though he was slowly losing his mind. He longed for the freedom of the outside world, for the feel of the breeze on his face and for the scent of the trees all around.

No matter how hard he tried to remember how he had ended up here, his mind continued to draw a blank. It was as though he had been plucked from his old life and placed in a glass prison without any warning or explanation.

He had no idea of how long he'd been trapped

in this sterile laboratory, but he knew that whoever had put him in the sealed beaker at least wanted to keep him alive. He was being sustained by the capsules dropped in via a tube at reasonable intervals. They contained both nutrition and hydration, and although they tasted bland and unappetising, he knew that he had to consume them in order to survive.

The two scientists who would come and go from the laboratory at various points throughout the day were the closest thing that Ke had to company in his predicament. They often took copious amounts of notes whilst referring to him as a mere subject. One was an obsessive middle-aged man with greying hair. The other was a younger female scientist. With soft features and with her hair tied up in a bushy, blonde ponytail, she seemed brighter in her overall demeanour. Nevertheless, both of them referred to Ke simply as Specimen Zero. They spoke about him in hushed tones, their voices barely audible over the thrum of the equipment.

Wires that had been embedded in his back snaked out from beneath his skin and into an ominous machine outside of his glass prison. Put in place to take readings on his emotions as well as his basic stats, they served as a constant reminder that within the confines of the laboratory, his life was not his own.

It was impossible for Ke to ignore the fact that he was being monitored, and as he sat there in despair, he felt like a puppet with strings attached to his every movement.

Chapter Three

Dr Fleming stood before the reinforced glass that separated him from the alien. The creature's beauty and grace was unparalleled, his very existence posing as a potential challenge to all human knowledge. Like a living opal, his shimmering, iridescent skin seemed to change colour with every subtle movement. Dr Fleming couldn't help but admire the subject.

"Ah, Specimen Zero," he murmured under his breath. "If only I could unlock the secrets of your spirituality. My name would be etched into the annals of history forever."

The scientist's eyes gleamed with naked ambition, betraying his need for adoration. He cleared his throat and addressed the alien directly.

"Can you understand me?"

The creature remained silent, watching him with vacant, unblinking eyes.

"Come on now," Dr Fleming coaxed, more urgently than he had intended. "Speak to me. Show me that my theories are not mere fancy."

Ke listened intently, weighing up his options. He understood the scientist's words, but was all too aware of the situation. By engaging with his captor, wouldn't it simply be giving this man what he wanted? The thought filled him with unease.

"Dr Fleming," Dr Carver said sternly as she entered the lab. "You know as well as I do that any true spiritual connection must be built on trust and mutual respect. It's not the kind of thing that can be forced."

"Dr Carver, please," Dr Fleming replied dismissively, refusing to take his eyes off the alien. "Science demands that we push the boundaries, even if it means bending our moral compass."

"*Your* moral compass, perhaps," she retorted, folding her arms. "Mine seems to be functioning just fine."

Dr Fleming let out a heavy sigh. As much as Dr Carver could be an annoyance, he still needed her to work on his research with him. It had always been difficult to find experienced researchers willing to commit to such demanding contracts.

Suppressing his frustration, he turned back to the alien and leaned in close to the glass.

"I do hope that you will converse with me. I promise that you have nothing to lose by doing so."

Ke remained silent, his empathetic nature causing him to feel pity for Dr Fleming's desperation. He wished to understand the man, but feared that speaking would only serve to strengthen the chains of his captivity. And so, for now, he chose to remain silent, watching as the scientist's face contorted with annoyance and disappointment.

A good while later, just when Ke thought it was safe to assume that he had – albeit to a small extent – acquired the upper hand, Dr Fleming tried again.

"Please, Specimen Zero," he implored with a forced sweetness as he tapped on the glass separating them. "I don't want to cause you any more distress than necessary. I just want to communicate. Please, just give me a sign that you understand."

Ke looked away from the persistent man, his eyes focusing on the sterile walls of the lab. As much as the vibrations from the scientist's constant tapping reverberated through his delicate senses and grated on his nerves, he was reluctant to let down his guard.

"Fine!" said Dr Fleming, huffing as he took a step back. "If you won't talk to me willingly, I'll just have to try something else. Even if it turns out that we don't speak the same language, the least you could do is open your mouth and say *something*."

The scientist reached impatiently into his lab coat pocket and pulled out a small device. It emitted a high-pitched whine.

With his finely-tuned senses unable to block anything out, the perpetual noise was unbearable to Ke. There was nothing he could tell himself that would give him the strength he needed to sit back and tolerate it.

"Stop!" he finally cried out, unable to bear the assault on his hearing any longer.

"Ah! You do speak!" Dr Fleming exclaimed, his face lighting up gleefully. "See? That wasn't so difficult, was it?"

Feeling triumphant in having secured a response from the alien, he smirked as he smugly shut off the device, which he then put back into his pocket.

Ke quivered with indignation. He regretted that he had given in to the maddening pain. Equally though, deep down, he knew that he couldn't have endured the torment any longer.

"Now we can begin our interviews," said Dr Fleming, ignoring the alien's evident reluctance. "I have so many questions that I want to ask about your spirituality, your beliefs, and how they compare to ours. This will be groundbreaking research, and perhaps you will learn a thing or two in the process."

"And what if I'd rather not talk?" the alien asked bitterly.

Dr Fleming shrugged, complacent in his rejection of the alien's concerns.

"You can trust me," he said. "I want nothing from you but your insight. Let us begin the interviews. I want to know everything about your spiritual beliefs and practices."

"Very well," the alien said with a sigh.

Having resigned himself to co-operating, Ke could only hope that by providing some information, it might eventually lead to him being set free.

"Excellent," said Dr Fleming, his eyes gleaming with anticipation.

Chapter Four

Dr Fleming leaned against one of the sterile metal counters of the laboratory, his arms folded across his chest as he observed the alien through the reinforced glass. As usual, his reflection stared back at him, his thin lips pressed together and his brow furrowed with determination.

Unresponsive to the one-man audience, with eyes firmly closed in a state of meditation, Ke sat cross-legged on the cold base of the glass beaker.

"Tell me, Specimen Zero," Dr Fleming began. "What is it that you miss most about your home?"

Ke opened his eyes slowly, fixing them on the scientist. For a moment, he hesitated, as if considering whether or not to answer.

Eventually, he spoke, his voice soft and melodic.

"I miss the feeling of unity, the connection with all living beings, and the harmony that comes from true understanding."

"Unity, you say? Interesting."

Dr Fleming scribbled something down on his clipboard, his eyes never leaving the alien.

"Your species must be quite different from ours," he said as he tapped his pen against his chin. "We humans tend to be more... fractured."

"Indeed," the alien replied, shifting his weight on the base of his glass floor. "It saddens me to think that there is such division among your people."

Dr Carver watched the exchange from the sidelines, her heart heavy with empathy for the captive being. She couldn't help but wonder what toll the ongoing confinement was taking on him. She also felt a pang of guilt for being complicit. She couldn't shake the notion that they were exploiting the alien's vulnerability for their own gain.

Chapter Five

The artificial lighting of the laboratory seemed to close in on Ke, suffocating him with its lifeless glare. As he sat on the cold glass of his beaker, in a feeble attempt to break the monotony, his long, slender digits tapped rhythmically against his muscular thighs.

The laboratory door slid open with a barely audible hiss, and in walked Dr Fleming, carrying a clipboard and pen.

"Good morning, Specimen Zero," he greeted, his voice dripping with a thinly veiled condescension. "You look well today."

Ke clenched his jaw and forced a smile, though it felt like a betrayal to his true emotions. His anger at being held captive boiled beneath the surface, but he pushed it away, reminding himself that co-operation was his best chance of one day being granted release.

"Thank you, Dr Fleming," he replied, his voice steady and calm despite his inner turmoil.

"Right then, shall we proceed with today's session?" the scientist asked.

His words were more in the manner of an instruction than a question as he pulled up a chair in front of the glass that formed the transparent wall between them.

"I have no doubt that you are surely an enlightened individual," Dr Fleming began. "All the same though, if there's anything that you don't understand, please do ask me to clarify."

"Very well," said Ke, his eyes narrowing slightly.

He knew that each question had probably been designed to measure his intelligence and probe his psyche. It bothered him that Dr Fleming seemed so sure that his answers would be of tremendous value. He was, after all, just one of his kind.

"Tell me, Specimen Zero," Dr Fleming said as he leaned back in his chair. "What are your thoughts on the nature of existence? Do you believe that reality is objective or subjective?"

It was an interesting question and one that Ke had thought about many times before.

"Reality is ultimately a matter of perception," he replied, his voice soft and contemplative. "We each experience the world through our own unique lens, which is shaped by our beliefs, experiences, and emotions. Thus, reality can be both objective and subjective, depending on the observer."

"Hmm..." Dr Fleming mused.

Ke watched as the scientist scribbled notes upon the stack of paper on his clipboard.

"And what of consciousness?" Dr Fleming asked. "Is it merely a product of complex biological processes, or does it transcend the physical realm?"

"Consciousness is more than just the sum of its parts," Ke replied, his voice gaining strength as he delved deeper into the topic. "It is an emergent property that arises from the interactions of the many components that make up our being. While it may have its roots in the physical, I believe it transcends the boundaries of the material world, reaching into the depths of the unknown."

Dr Fleming raised an eyebrow, clearly intrigued by this response.

"Fascinating. And how do you perceive the concept of morality? Is it an innate aspect of existence, or is it purely a social construct?"

Ke paused for a moment to gather his thoughts. It was a struggle for him to get past the irony of how the man holding him captive wanted to talk about morality. Nevertheless, he reminded himself that perhaps his freedom would come sooner should the scientist reach a point where all possible questions had been exhausted.

"I would say that morality is not black and white," Ke answered. "It seems to exist within the shades of grey that colour our existence. It is both innate and constructed, influenced by our biology, culture, and personal experiences. Ultimately, it is a reflection of our collective journey through life, constantly evolving and adapting to the challenges we face."

A hint of frustration crossed Dr Fleming's face. He was almost displeased that the questions seemed so easy for the alien. He could barely admit to himself that he would need to put some considerable thought into how best to record and collate the subject's responses.

"Alright then, let's discuss the nature of suffering," he said. "Do you believe it serves a purpose, or is it simply a cruel by-product of existence?"

Once again, Ke was taken aback by the audacity of Dr Fleming's line of questioning. The very man who was the cause of his current suffering was set on interviewing him about the overall concept in a more general sense. Despite the fact that Ke was finding their conversation stimulating, he couldn't help but be disgusted by this.

The alien sighed, determined to give a good answer.

"Although suffering can be difficult to comprehend, it is an essential aspect of life. It can teach us valuable lessons, fostering growth and transformation. Suffering is not a punishment, but rather an opportunity for us to discover our true strength, resilience, and compassion."

Furrowing his brow, Dr Fleming's grip tightened around his pen as he struggled to get his head around the alien's response.

"And what of death?" he asked. "Is it merely the end of existence, or does it serve a higher purpose?"

"Death is a natural part of the cycle of life," Ke replied, his voice imbued with a quiet reverence. "It is not something to be feared, but rather embraced as a transition from one state of being to another. Whilst the physical body may cease to exist, the essence of who we are – our consciousness, our memories, our emotions – continues on in some form, whether it is through the impact we have made on others, or the legacy we leave behind."

"Your answers are impressive, Specimen Zero," said Dr Fleming in a sickly-sweet tone. "Very impressive indeed."

Like many of his kind, Ke had always felt at one with himself and the world around him. He didn't need any human to be impressed by what came naturally to him. He just wanted to maintain his sanity whilst in captivity, but more than that, to go home. Still though, he took a strange comfort in how despite the fact that he was the one trapped in a glass beaker, it seemed to be Dr Fleming who was confined – by the limitations of his own mind.

A tense silence filled the room, the air thick with unspoken thoughts and emotions. For a brief moment, Dr Fleming looked as though he was about to ask more questions, but instead, he simply gave a graceful nod before pushing back his chair and standing up.

"That will be all for now, Specimen Zero. We'll continue this discussion another time."

With that, he turned and walked out of the lab, once again leaving Ke alone with nothing but the oppressive blandness of the timeless space.

Chapter Six

Ke's head tilted slightly as he noticed some movement in the glass terrarium next to his beaker. Inside the larger enclosure, various specimens of small, insect-like creatures crawled and fluttered among the foliage. He gently tapped on the glass of his own confinement with one of his long, slender fingers, and watched curiously as the tiny beings scurried away, seeking refuge under leaves or within the crevices of one of the many pieces of bark.

"Dr Fleming," Ke said as he turned to engage with the irritable scientist. "Why do you keep these smaller lifeforms?"

"Ah, those are for study as well," Dr Fleming replied dismissively. "They are nothing compared to you, of course. Mere insects."

"Yet they too are alive, are they not?" Ke queried. "Every single one of them has their own unique role within the web of existence."

"Perhaps," Dr Fleming conceded.

The scientist seemed to have little interest in discussing the matter further. Instead, he busied himself by adjusting some dials on a nearby console, leaving Ke to contemplate the tiny lives contained within the terrarium.

In that moment, Ke felt a pang of empathy for the insects, their delicate wings and fragile bodies trapped in this artificial world, far from the freedom of open skies and sunlit meadows. He longed to reach into the terrarium, to cradle them in his hands and set them free, but knew that even if such actions were possible, they would only anger his captor.

As he continued to gaze at the items surrounding his glass prison, Ke's attention was drawn to a scale model of an old English church. Carefully crafted from aged wood and stained glass, the intricate details on the model were astounding – the weathered stone arches, the ornate wooden carvings, and the beautifully painted windows depicting scenes from sacred texts. The way in which it was both mesmerising and foreign to Ke was such that it sparked a deep curiosity within him. He wanted to know more about the purpose and significance of such a structure.

"Dr Fleming," he said, his voice soft with wonder. "This model... Is it a representation of something significant to your people?"

"Ah, yes," Dr Fleming replied, the pride in his voice unmistakable. "A place for worship and reflection, it's a replica of a church from my home country."

"Interesting," Ke mused. "We have nothing like this on my planet. And yet, there is an undeniable beauty to it."

The alien's eyes lingered on the images of saints and angels, their ethereal forms bathed in the warm glow of a nearby lamp.

"Indeed," Dr Fleming agreed. "I'm glad you think so."

Ke looked longingly at the church model before turning his attention back to his captor. Deep in his soul, an ember of hope began to kindle – perhaps these earthly symbols of faith and love could hold the key to helping him understand the nature of human spiritual inclinations, and ultimately, to finding a way out of his captivity.

Chapter Seven

The following day, Ke found himself once again drawn to the old English church model. He marvelled at the intricate craftsmanship and at how each piece seemed to have a purpose. The fluorescent laboratory lighting served to cast shadows upon the miniature structure. As he studied it, a sense of longing stirred within him.

"Dr Fleming," he began, careful to keep his tone respectful. "I cannot help but feel a connection with this church model. Could you tell me more about the symbols on it? What do they represent?"

Dr Fleming set aside his clipboard and approached, studying the alien with a hint of admiration in his eyes.

"Well, each symbol has its own meaning tied

to our religious beliefs," he explained as he pointed to a cross. "This one, for instance, represents the crucifixion and resurrection of Jesus Christ."

Ke's eyes widened in fascination.

"We have a similar concept on my planet – a belief in rebirth after death."

A memory flashed before Ke's eyes: a ceremony held beneath the stars, where loved ones gathered to honour the passing of an elder, their soul ascending into the cosmos.

"Really?" said Dr Fleming, his tone one of surprise. "That is quite intriguing. It's not often that we find such common ground between species."

"Indeed," Ke agreed.

As much as he hated his captivity, Ke had begun to enjoy some of his conversations with Dr Fleming. He was learning so much, and the newfound knowledge was like a beacon, guiding him towards a deeper understanding of both human spirituality and his own.

"What about the other symbols?" the alien

asked. "Do they all hold such profound meanings?"

"Most of them, yes," Dr Fleming replied, pointing out different symbols as he explained their significance. "For example, the dove represents peace and hope, while the lamb symbolises innocence and purity."

As Ke listened, he couldn't help but draw parallels between the earthly symbols in front of him and the various rituals and beliefs he'd known back on his home planet. He realised that, despite the difference between humans and his own species, there was a universal yearning for solace and meaning in the face of life's many challenges.

"Thank you for sharing this with me, Dr Fleming," Ke said sincerely, a sense of awe resonating within him. "I find it comforting to know that, even in our darkest moments, we are not alone in our search for understanding."

Dr Fleming nodded, visibly pleased by the alien's interest in human culture.

"You're quite welcome, Specimen Zero. I'm glad you can appreciate the depth of our beliefs."

As they continued their conversation, Ke felt an unexpected kinship with the humans who had created such beautiful symbols of faith, hope, and love. Though he remained trapped in the lab, the knowledge he was gaining from these observations helped to nourish his spirit and strengthen his resolve. Perhaps one day, through understanding and empathy, he could even find a way to bridge the gap between their worlds in order to secure his freedom.

Chapter Eight

As the days turned to weeks, Ke's fascination with the church model began to wane and was replaced by a growing restlessness. He was so weary of his glass enclosure, his disproportionately large feet tapping rhythmically against the cold base of it. The overhead lights cast eerie shadows on his peridot-tinged skin as he traced patterns in the thin layer of condensation upon the glass.

He turned to address Dr Fleming, who was absorbed in scribbling notes at a nearby workbench.

"Dr Fleming, I must ask you something important," he said. "How long do you intend to keep me here?"

The question hung in the air like an unwelcome guest, but Dr Fleming pretended not to notice.

His tired eyes remained fixed on the pages before him, his pen scratching insistently across the paper.

"Specimen Zero, you must understand that your presence here is vital to the advancement of human knowledge," he replied without looking up. "There is so much we can learn from you."

"Indeed, but what of my own life? My family, my friends – they must be worried sick about me," Ke said, desperation creeping into his voice. "I have co-operated with you. I have shared information about my culture and beliefs. Surely there must be a way for us to continue this exchange without me being held captive."

"Perhaps," Dr Fleming conceded, finally glancing up from his work. "But until I'm convinced that releasing you will not backfire on me somehow, you must remain here."

The accusation felt quite hurtful to Ke. It served as a stark reminder that no matter how gracious and how polite he had tried to be, humans would always see him as something other than them; as a being too dangerous, and too different, to be trusted.

"Do you not trust me?" Ke asked as he quivered in indignation. "Have I not shown you time and time again that I am a creature of peace? I simply wish to return home and live my life. I would even be happy to continue a correspondence with you, should it prove to be useful to your research."

Ke wasn't sure if he truly believed in committing to what he had just promised. He had, after all, been imprisoned by Dr Fleming against his will. All the same though, he had found some of their conversations fascinating and had been enjoying learning about the human take on spirituality.

"It's possible that your intentions may be pure," Dr Fleming said, his voice cold and detached. "Nevertheless, your kind possesses abilities far beyond our comprehension. The risk is too great."

"Risk?" Ke echoed, his eyes narrowing as he focused intently on the scientist. "Is it not a greater risk to keep me here against my will? What if my family come looking for me?"

"Let them come," Dr Fleming said, scoffing. "We'll be prepared."

Ke shook his head, dismay evident in his every movement. He knew that despite their moments of shared understanding, Dr Fleming could not see past the ambition and fear that seemed to drive so many of his actions.

"Very well, Dr Fleming," he said quietly, resignation settling over him like a shroud. "But know this: I hope that one day, in the not-too-distant future, you will learn the lessons of empathy and compassion that you so desperately need."

Ke ached for the life he had lost, the freedom he craved, and the loved ones waiting for him among the stars.

"Time will tell, Specimen Zero," Dr Fleming replied, his expression unreadable. "Time will tell."

Chapter Nine

The stale air in the lab carried the pungent smell of disinfectant. Mingling with the metallic scent of machinery, day in and day out, it was maddening.

"Focus," Ke whispered to himself as he closed his eyes. "Remember who you are."

His mind drifted back to a time before the lab, when he was free to explore the vast expanse of the universe. He recalled the warmth of his home planet's sun, the gentle rustle of leaves in the wind, and the sound of laughter echoing through the air. It was there that he had first developed his beliefs – the importance of peace, compassion, and unity among all living beings.

"Specimen Zero, are you ok?" Dr Carver's voice broke through the alien's reverie.

Despite the clinical detachment that she tried to maintain, she was clearly concerned.

"Forgive me, Dr Carver," Ke replied, opening his eyes. "I was... remembering."

"Your past?" she asked, her curiosity piqued.

"Indeed," he said.

His thoughts turned to the countless worlds he had visited and the many beings he had encountered, each one unique in their own way.

"I believe that every lifeform holds a piece of the universal truth," he said. "But in their infinite beauty, they can only be at peace when free to roam."

"An admirable perspective," Dr Carver acknowledged, though her eyes were clouded with sadness. "I wish I could say that everyone here shared your beliefs."

"Dr Fleming certainly does not," Ke remarked bitterly, recalling the arrogant sneer on the scientist's face. "He has no concern for the lives he disrupts or destroys in his quest for knowledge."

"Dr Fleming is... complicated," Dr Carver admitted, hesitating. "Sometimes I still have hope, that if shown the right path, even he could learn to embrace a more compassionate approach in his methods."

"Perhaps," Ke mused.

Privately, he doubted Dr Carver's optimism. He had seen firsthand the nonchalance that Dr Fleming was capable of. He felt certain that the man would stop at nothing to achieve his goals – no matter the cost.

"Dr Carver," he said suddenly, struck by another memory from his past. "On my travels, I encountered a race of beings who possessed an extraordinary gift – the ability to heal others with a mere touch. They believed that this power came from their connection to the universe, and they used it to help those in need."

"Amazing," said the scientist, her expression alight with astonishment. "If only we could harness such a power, imagine the good we could do."

"Indeed," Ke agreed solemnly.

It saddened him that such wonders were forever beyond the reach of even the kindest humans.

Chapter Ten

Carl, the burly and affable security guard assigned to watch over the research facility, cautiously entered the laboratory. He had been warned by the scientists that the alien they referred to as Specimen Zero was off-limits to all other personnel. Nevertheless, he was curious and wanted to see the creature for himself.

He scanned the room with a trained eye, taking in the bank of computers, the beakers and test tubes, and the complicated pieces of equipment that he didn't recognise. The alien in the beaker stood out from it all, of course. A distinguished thin figure with green skin and large sharp teeth, it was facing away from the laboratory door. Carl was convinced that he could feel the alien's presence throughout the entire room – he likened it to the feeling of a slight current in the air that seemed to hum and vibrate with its otherness.

As he continued to stare at the alien, he couldn't help but tilt his head curiously – as though trying to figure out the purpose and motives of such a strange being. It was a question he knew he'd never be able to answer, but it still excited him to consider the possibilities.

He took a step closer, and as he did, the alien shifted around to meet his gaze. The very air around its glass beaker seemed to become more charged with its presence.

As it suddenly dawned on Carl that he could be standing at the precipice of something unknown yet earth-shatteringly significant, his pulse quickened. He was both fascinated and scared, but eventually he collected himself enough to give the alien a respectful bow.

"Hey there, alien dude," he said softly, his voice warm and kind.

He couldn't take his eyes off the creature. He was mesmerised by its strange form and by the incredibly powerful presence it seemed to exude – one that seemed to carry secrets and knowledge that could potentially change the way humans viewed the universe.

He stepped closer, feeling a strong urge to reach out and touch the creature, even though the secure beaker made the prospect of such contact impossible. Instead, he pressed his meaty hand against the glass, observing the alien's curious nature. As he noticed the approachable innocence shining in its eyes, he wondered what secrets it could tell him if only he knew how to communicate with it.

"Carl!" Dr Fleming snapped as he entered the room, clearly irritated by the guard's interest in the alien. "This is not the time for idle distractions. We have important work to do."

"Sorry, Doc," Carl said absently.

He was too enchanted by the alien to be startled or particularly engaged with Dr Fleming's chastisement. Eventually though, he snapped out of his trance and backed away from the glass, his gaze lingering on the alien for a moment longer before reluctantly leaving to return to his post.

Dr Carver then entered the lab.

"Is everything ok?" she asked.

"No, it most certainly is not," Dr Fleming complained. "Specimen Zero is not here for the purpose of entertainment. Who does that idiot think he is, coming in here and treating the place like a zoo?"

"Maybe Specimen Zero appreciated the company," Dr Carver mused. "He must be missing his loved ones back home. Perhaps there are things we could do that would make life more bearable for him whilst he stays here with us. I'm sure it could be done in a way that doesn't compromise any vital consistencies that are required for the project."

The young woman couldn't help but feel a spark of hope at the thought of doing anything possible to help make the alien feel less alone.

"I could create a space for him; somewhere that would feel safe and comfortable, ideally resembling something closer to his home environment," she continued. "I could provide enrichment activities and distractions, like games and entertainment to help stimulate his mind. I could..."

"Why complicate things?" Dr Fleming cut in. "This is science, not storytime."

"But don't you think it would be good to treat Specimen Zero with a bit more dignity? Don't you think it would be nice to let him have some home comforts?"

Dr Fleming scoffed, his eyes never leaving the intricate web of data he was studying.

"I have full confidence in my methodology, Dr Carver. I am not prepared to make drastic changes at this stage, especially when with the current set-up, I am still able to acquire useful data."

Dr Carver's face twisted in disgust as she watched Dr Fleming pore over his findings. Evidently convinced that his chosen approach was equally valid and acceptable, he had his sights set on fame, and on securing his place in history.

58

Chapter Eleven

As Ke continued to wearily look around, he became acutely aware of the laboratory's sterility. The sharp tang of disinfectant was a far cry from the warm, earthy aromas of his own world, and the rich scents of fertile soil and lush vegetation that he had once taken for granted. The whirr of machinery was nothing like the song of free birds soaring elegantly across the soft blue sky. His heart ached with longing for his home as the cold glass walls of his prison seemed to close in around him.

"Please, Dr Fleming," he said sadly. "Will you let me leave? If not today, then at least when you've got what you need from me?"

The scientist studied the alien for a moment, his eyes narrowing as if weighing up the options before him.

"I cannot make any promises, Specimen Zero," he said with a tired sigh. "But I will consider it."

"Please," Ke begged, the word escaping him like a breath. "I miss my home, my family. Every day that passes, I feel as though a part of me is slipping away."

"I understand," Dr Fleming said quietly, though his expression remained impassive. "But you must also understand the position I am in. I can't give up in the middle of a research project – not when I'm learning so much about you every day. Besides, I have a reputation to maintain."

Ke nodded, knowing that there was little else he could say. He then retreated back into his own thoughts. In the cold, sterile environment that threatened to extinguish his last flickers of hope, he was consumed by his need to return home.

Chapter Twelve

Despite having been told to keep well away, Carl once again entered the laboratory. He was itching to get a closer look at the alien. Knowing that Dr Fleming was possessive of the creature, he had made sure to time his visit just right. Only when the coast was clear did he excitedly stride in.

Holding a small bag in his hands, the security guard was eager to share its contents with the alien. He had spent the previous evening scouring his apartment for items that might be of intrigue: a colourful rubber ball, a shiny metal spoon, and even a few chocolate bars that he thought the creature might enjoy.

Not only was Carl filled with a sense of purpose, but with a desire to make a connection with the alien. It excited him so much to think that just maybe, there was a possibility of being able to share a real friendship with an otherworldly species.

"Look what I got for ya," he whispered excitedly.

Keen for the alien to see it, he held up the bag in front of the glass.

Although it was clear to Ke that Carl deemed his intelligence to be relatively low, he found his approach to be endearing and thoughtful. As misguided as the security guard's assumption was, it was evident that he meant well. Such was the sincerity of his actions that Ke could sense the man's genuine desire for friendship.

Carl couldn't help but smile at the alien. With a mixture of wonder and affection, he had been looking forward to interacting with the creature.

No such luck though. As soon as he started to delve into his bag of goodies, he could hear footsteps coming towards the lab.

He quickly backed away from the alien's glass beaker and cleared his throat nervously. He tried to think of something to say – anything that would explain why he was in the lab.

"Carl!" Dr Fleming snapped as he tried to maintain control over his anger. "What exactly do you think you're doing?! Specimen Zero is not here for your amusement!"

His expression a combination of surprise and defiance, Carl turned around to face his volatile colleague.

"Sorry, Doc. Specimen Zero is just so awesome. And anyway, he seems pretty harmless," he protested. "I've never seen anything like it. I just couldn't resist. Besides, I think he likes it when I talk to him."

Carl looked back at the alien, who had now chosen to remain impassive for his own good.

"Don't interfere with my work," Dr Fleming reiterated sternly. "Specimen Zero is not a pet. It's here for research purposes only."

"Right, right," Carl muttered uncomfortably.

"Your job is to guard this facility, not to interfere with my research!" Dr Fleming continued, his voice growing louder. "You've got no idea what you could be doing to the data we've collected so far!"

Pulling her white coat on, Dr Carver promptly entered the lab. Still with a bite of her sandwich in her mouth, she had heard the commotion. With Dr Fleming having been so on edge recently, she hadn't thought twice about cutting her lunch break short.

"Dr Fleming, please," she interjected. "We should consider the possibility that Carl's approach could lead to valuable insights. After all, there could prove to be some interesting links between spirituality and social interaction."

Dr Fleming glared at the younger scientist, his anger now directed at her as well as at Carl.

"Dr Carver, I can't believe that you're entertaining this nonsense," he said furiously. "This is a scientific research facility, not a playground. Our goal is to study the alien's spirituality, not to entertain it!"

"But don't you think that connecting with Specimen Zero on a playful level could help us to better understand its spirituality?" she reasoned, her tone firm yet diplomatic. "Think of it as another method of data collection."

"I agree," Carl butted in, his gaze still fixed on the silent alien. "It doesn't seem right to keep it locked up without any form of stimulation. It's a living being, not just a lab rat."

"Enough!" Dr Fleming barked, his face red with fury. "I will not allow my research to be compromised by misplaced compassion or curiosity. If you insist on continuing this charade, Carl, I will have no choice but to see to it that your employment here is terminated."

Carl clenched his jaw, his eyes meeting Dr Fleming's in a silent challenge. He glanced briefly at Dr Carver, who looked torn between her loyalty to her job and her own ethical concerns.

"Fine," Carl muttered through gritted teeth, stepping back from the glass. "But know that I don't agree with how you're treating it."

"Your agreement is not required," Dr Fleming said, asserting his authority with undisguised contempt.

As Carl strode indignantly out of the laboratory, Dr Carver sighed, her gaze shifting between Dr Fleming and Specimen Zero, whose sad, unblinking eyes seemed to plead for understanding. Observing how the alien bowed its head in defeat, she couldn't shake the unsettling feeling that they were all on the brink of something catastrophic – and that their actions would ultimately determine whether they would emerge as heroes or villains.

Chapter Thirteen

The laboratory's vast cavern of cold steel stretched out before Ke like a soulless eternity. The bright fluorescent lights buzzed overhead, casting harsh shadows amidst the labyrinthine maze of equipment. Monitors blinked and beeped as they displayed an endless stream of data, while machines whirred tirelessly, their purposes hidden behind glass casings and metal panels.

Trapped in his glass beaker at the centre of the mechanical jungle, Ke's eyes flickered with a mixture of fear and desperation as they reflected the illuminations of his environment in a dazzling array of colour.

His delicate fingers deftly traced along the cold surface of the glass, searching for any weakness in the structure. His thoughts of escape had been growing more prominent. He knew that

Dr Fleming had full control of his fate. Having tried countless times to appeal to the human's better nature, he had continued to be met with nothing but indifference.

"Dr Fleming, please," Ke whispered, his voice tinged with a lilting melody that seemed almost unnatural. "I ask only for your understanding, your compassion."

Dr Fleming scoffed as he continued to tap away at a keyboard attached to the machinery surrounding the alien's glass prison.

"Compassion?" the scientist said incredulously. "As a researcher, it's my duty to find out everything I can about you."

Ke looked into the man's remorseless eyes, his own pupils dilating with terror. He fought to maintain the serenity that had long been fundamental to his wellbeing, but the relentless acceleration of his pulse threatened to shatter his resolve. It was clear that Dr Fleming viewed him as nothing more than a means to an end.

The alien pressed his palms against the glass as if trying to will himself through the barrier.

"*Please*," he begged, his voice quivering with the weight of his desperation. "There must be another way."

As every minute turned to hours in his sterile chamber, Ke began to wonder if there was any hope left to be found.

Chapter Fourteen

Dr Fleming stood triumphantly by the secured beaker that held Specimen Zero, his face reflecting both pride and a thirst for validation. The alien creature was slumped against the glass, his otherworldly eyes half-closed in what seemed like resignation.

"Observe, Dr Carver," said Dr Fleming with a grandiose wave of his hand. "My latest findings are now at the point where we can begin to look for patterns and correlations that have never been found before."

Dr Carver approached the glass beaker hesitantly. Her eyes flickered between the charts and graphs displayed on the monitors and the defeated-looking alien, her brow furrowing with concern.

"I can see the data," she began cautiously, "But how did you reach these conclusions?"

"My novel approach is proving to be fruitful," Dr Fleming answered, not bothering to hide his arrogance. "I've exposed Specimen Zero to various religious texts and symbols, monitoring his neurological and physiological responses. The results so far have been extraordinary. The subject has exhibited elevated levels of endorphins and serotonin when presented with certain spiritual concepts, suggesting a deep-rooted connection to a higher power."

As Dr Fleming revelled in his own brilliance, Dr Carver couldn't help but notice the callous treatment of the alien. She glanced at the protruding wires that snaked out from his back, the bruises of their insertions marring the creature's ethereal skin where the cold metal had been forced into its flesh. A pang of unease settled in her stomach, intensifying as she realised the extent of her colleague's obsession with proving his self-proclaimed superiority.

"Dr Fleming, I can understand the scientific merit of what you seek to achieve, but have you truly considered the consequences of your research?" she asked, her voice wavering with concern. "I'm thinking specifically in terms of Specimen Zero's wellbeing."

"Wellbeing?" Dr Fleming quipped, his eyes narrowing with disdain. "This is groundbreaking research, Dr Carver. Not only will it revolutionise our understanding of extraterrestrial life, but of the nature of spirituality itself."

Dr Carver bit her lip, struggling to contain her growing unease. She looked once more at Specimen Zero, whose haunted eyes seemed to plead for mercy.

As the alien's gaze remained fixed on hers, a silent connection forged between them, and in that brief moment, she couldn't shake the feeling that they were on the precipice of something far more significant than what Dr Fleming's vanity could comprehend.

"Dr Fleming," she said firmly, her voice steady despite the uncertainty churning within her. "Moving forward, I believe it's essential that we prioritise Specimen Zero's welfare. We must remember that we are dealing with a sentient being, not just a test subject."

"Sentimentality has no place in science, Dr Carver," Dr Fleming snapped, his expression darkening. "If you cannot handle the rigors of this research, perhaps you should reconsider your place in this project."

Chapter Fifteen

The heavy steel door slid open with a hollow, grating sound. As Dr Carver entered the laboratory, her footsteps echoed throughout the vast room. She paused for a moment, her gaze flicking between Specimen Zero and Dr Fleming.

"Dr Fleming, I've been meaning to talk to you again about our... guest," she began hesitantly, her concern evident in the furrow of her brow.

"Can't you see that I'm busy?" Dr Fleming muttered condescendingly, not bothering to look up from his work.

Unwilling to be deterred, Dr Carver pressed on.

"It's unethical to keep him here against his will. It's cruel."

Dr Fleming grunted in annoyance before finally turning to face his younger colleague. His eyes cold and unyielding, he had long grown tired of his methods being questioned by her.

"I won't let your bleeding heart stand in the way of progress," he said bluntly.

From the distance of his glass prison, Ke watched the heated exchange, his hopes sinking at the reality of just how ruthless Dr Fleming truly was. He felt a deep sense of unease settling in his chest, like the slow emergence of a toxic fog.

Is my suffering just another variable in his grand experiment? How far is he willing to go in order to satisfy his curiosity?

Clipboard in hand, Dr Carver waltzed out of the lab to work alone. As Dr Fleming turned back to his work, Ke continued to ponder his predicament. At the very core of his being, he knew that escape would come at a terrible cost – not only to himself, but to those whose lives he would have to endanger in his quest for freedom.

In view of the chaos it could unleash should I try to escape, would it be right to prioritise my own life?

In a whirlwind of terror and uncertainty that threatened to consume him, Ke's thoughts raced like a storm. With his mind teetering on the edge of despair as he listened to the rhythm of motors and the murmur of voices just beyond the glass, he knew that his decision could no longer be delayed.

Chapter Sixteen

D r Carver was working alone in the laboratory, her pristine white lab coat billowing out like a cape behind her as she wandered around. Deep in thought, she examined a length of notes that had been scrawled hastily in blue biro against a clipboard.

Watching the sight before him, Ke couldn't help but smile to himself. He had been eagerly awaiting the chance to talk to Dr Carver without Dr Fleming there to judge every word.

"Dr Carver," said Ke, his voice trembling as he spoke. "What do you think of Dr Fleming's research?"

In the deathly silence of the laboratory, Ke could feel the kind scientist's gaze upon him. Despite the boldness of his question, he didn't dare to meet her eyes. He just couldn't unshackle himself from the shame that had attached itself to him ever since he had been brought into this cold, sterile environment.

"Specimen Zero," she began hesitantly, weighing her words carefully. "I... I don't agree with his methods. But sometimes, progress requires sacrifice."

Ke sensed the woman's deep-rooted discomfort. It served to fuel his own anxieties.

"And if that sacrifice is me? If it is my life on the line?"

"Then we must weigh the potential benefits against the cost," Dr Carver replied, her voice barely audible over the steady hum of machinery and the distant echo of footsteps in the corridor. "But please know that I will do everything in my power to ensure your safety, Specimen Zero."

"Everything?" Ke whispered.

He could taste the bitterness of uncertainty on his tongue as the air grew heavy around him. Laden with the scent of sweat and unspoken fears, it hung between them like a shroud.

"*Everything*," Dr Carver repeated, her voice firmer. "You have my word."

Suddenly grasping the magnitude of their conversation, Ke could only hope that the woman would stay true to her promise.

"Thank you, Dr Carver," he muttered humbly.

"Specimen Zero, I..."

Her words were cut off by the sudden appearance of Dr Fleming at the laboratory door.

"Ah, Dr Carver... there you are," he said, his voice dripping with false warmth. "I was just looking for you. We have a lot to discuss."

As the two scientists drifted away, their voices fading into a murmur, Ke was left alone with the crushing weight of his fears. Exhausted from the emotional turmoil of it all, as shadows deepened in the corners of the laboratory, he yearned for the warmth of home.

Chapter Seventeen

Ke closed his eyes and focused on the rhythmic cadences of his breathing. As he drew in the stagnant air of the laboratory and exhaled the pain that consumed him, he burned with the desire for freedom. Nevertheless, thoughts of the harm that he might have to cause to others in order to obtain it continued to weigh heavily upon his conscience. It was a moral dilemma that tore at the very essence of his being.

As the laboratory lights flickered intrusively overhead, casting their cold, sterile glow across the room, Dr Carver continued to stare at the alien's glass beaker. Her eyes narrowed in concern, and her fingers tightened around the clipboard she was holding – her knuckles were beginning to turn white as she clenched it in frustration.

"Dr Fleming," she called out, her voice firm, yet tinged with unease. "I need to speak with you about something rather important."

Dr Fleming turned away from the array of monitors displaying intricate graphs and streams of data, a look of irritation crossing his face.

"What is it now, Dr Carver?" he snapped as he brushed a stray lock of hair away from his forehead. "Can't you see that I'm busy?"

"This is important," she retorted, stepping forward to confront him directly. "Have you ever stopped to consider the ethical implications of your actions?"

"Ethics?" he said, rolling his eyes. "This is science, Dr Carver, not a church sermon. Besides, you and I both know that I am on the verge of a career-defining discovery here."

"By keeping an innocent being captive?" Dr Carver shot back, her voice rising. "Look at him!"

She gestured towards the alien, who had opened his eyes and was observing the exchange with a deep sadness in his gaze.

"He's suffering, Dr Fleming. This is wrong."

Dr Fleming crossed the room in three quick strides to stand toe-to-toe with his colleague.

"Wrong?" he said, his tone cutting and cold. "Let me tell you something: this *creature* is invaluable to our research. He's a goldmine for scientific discovery!"

The way Dr Fleming spat the word 'creature' with such contempt caused Ke to shudder. He could feel the tension between the two scientists, their emotions swirling around him like a vortex. He didn't doubt that Dr Carver was concerned for his wellbeing, but he couldn't help but question whether her compassion would be enough to sway the mind of a man who seemed so intent on maintaining control.

"Dr Fleming," Dr Carver said, her eyes never leaving his. "You're not only hurting Specimen Zero, you're hurting yourself too. Don't you see that?"

For a brief moment, a flicker of doubt seemed to pass over Dr Fleming's face. But then he shook his head, dismissing the thought as quickly as it had arrived. His expression hardened, and he squared his shoulders, standing tall and obstinate.

"Enough!" he barked. "I don't want to hear another word about this. Get back to work, Amelia."

Dr Carver studied the monitor displaying Specimen Zero's latest test results. The buzz coming from the machines was punctuated by the steady beep of a heart rate monitor. She clenched her jaw, her eyes scanning the data with increasing concern.

"Dr Fleming," she called out, not bothering to hide the urgency in her voice. "You need to see this."

Dr Fleming looked up from his own workstation, irritation flashing across his features at the interruption. He begrudgingly made his way over to Dr Carver, his lab coat swishing as he moved.

"What is it now?" he snapped, his patience wearing thin.

"Look at these readings," she said as she pointed to the screen, her eyes never leaving the data. "Specimen Zero's stress levels are off the charts. We're causing him irreparable harm, and for what? To prove your theories?"

"We've been over this," Dr Fleming insisted, his voice almost a growl. "When all's said and done, Specimen Zero is simply a test subject. A little stress won't hurt him."

"Look at him!" Dr Carver demanded as she pointed at the glass separating them from the creature. "He's wasting away in there."

"I'm convinced that Specimen Zero is stronger than you give him credit for," Dr Fleming said nonchalantly.

As the man combed a hand through his thinning hair, Dr Carver's eyes brimmed with concern as she looked at Specimen Zero, his once-lustrous skin now dull and lifeless.

"Your concern is touching, but misguided," Dr Fleming continued. "This creature, this *specimen*, could be the key to unlocking secrets beyond our comprehension. Its spiritual abilities alone could potentially revolutionise our understanding of the universe! We can't afford to let emotions cloud our judgment."

"Emotions? This isn't about emotions. It's

about *ethics*!" Dr Carver insisted, the colour rising in her cheeks. "What we're doing to Specimen Zero is *wrong*. Don't you see? The longer we keep him here, the more we risk losing everything that makes him unique. His spirituality, his extraordinary insight – they could be lost forever. Besides, there is no scientific basis for keeping him in captivity any longer. We have gathered enough data to last us a lifetime. It's time to release him."

"Release him?!" Dr Fleming said furiously. "Do you honestly think that I would let all my hard work go to waste?"

"Is your pride worth more than this creature's life?" Dr Carver retorted, her own anger flaring up. "As researchers, it's our duty to study and understand, not to destroy."

She bit her lip, trying to maintain control of her feelings.

"You're being incredibly naive," Dr Fleming snapped, his voice rising in pitch. "This conversation is over. Specimen Zero stays, and that's final!"

Dr Carver stared at Specimen Zero, deeply upset for the creature trapped behind the glass.

She couldn't shake the feeling that he was running out of time, and that if they didn't act soon, the magnificent being before her would surely perish.

Determined to hold her ground, she glared at Dr Fleming with steely resolve.

"You're letting your pride blind you to what's right in front of us," she said as she gestured towards the alien. "Can't you see the harm we're doing to Specimen Zero?"

"You're allowing yourself to become too attached, Dr Carver. It's unbecoming of a scientist. I will not stand here and be lectured on the nature of science by someone who can't separate fact from sentiment!"

Once again Dr Carver bit her lip, this time struggling to hold back tears.

Refusing to be intimidated, with a heavy sigh, she turned on her heel and walked out of the lab, the tension of the heated argument pressing down upon her.

Chapter Eighteen

Dr Carver's footsteps echoed throughout the pristine, surgical corridors. A knot tightened in her chest as she choked back the tears that threatened to spill.

"Dr Carver!"

It was Dr Fleming. His voice – laced with anger and disbelief – rang out as he trailed along several steps behind her. She could feel his eyes boring into her back.

Unwilling to let him see her vulnerability, she refused to turn around and face him.

"Leave me be," she muttered, her jaw clenched as she fought back her emotions.

"Surely you don't want to walk out over this?" he said. "Our work together, our partnership?

And all because you've become attached to a… a specimen?"

"He's a living being, Arthur, with feelings and thoughts just like ours. He deserves better than to be treated as a mere tool in your overzealous methods."

Dr Carver's resolve crumbled as she spun around to face her colleague. Tears blurred her vision, but she could still make out the shock on his face. He had never seen her cry before.

"Emotions have no place in science," he replied sternly, his features hardening once more. "You're letting your sentimentality cloud your judgment."

"Perhaps my judgment is the only thing keeping us from becoming monsters," she whispered to herself, her voice trembling.

As Dr Fleming's footsteps disappeared into the distance, the anticipation for what could come next hung thick in the air like the static charge before a storm.

***

Dr Carver slammed the door of the restroom

behind her, her heart pounding in her chest as the aftershocks of the argument with Dr Fleming still coursed through her veins. The grey tiles and soft floral scent of the small space provided a stark contrast to the fury bubbling inside her. She could still feel the heat of his breath on her face, the force of his words as he'd dismissed her concerns for Specimen Zero like swatting away an annoying fly.

Her knuckles turned white as her hands gripped the edge of the porcelain sink. Her anger flared again as she replayed Dr Fleming's condescending tone in her head. Her reflection in the mirror showed the redness in her cheeks and the fire in her eyes. Trying to calm herself, she took a deep breath.

"Get it together, Amelia," she whispered.

Focusing on her reflection, she willed herself to regain control. She couldn't ignore the enormity of her responsibility towards Specimen Zero. She couldn't abandon him; he needed her. If she were to walk out on this project now, who else would care enough to ensure his wellbeing?

"Damn you, Arthur Fleming," she said through gritted teeth.

She was all too aware that for all his brilliance, Dr Fleming's vanity and ambition blinded him to the suffering of the very creature that held the key to so much knowledge, so much wisdom. And yet, she knew that if she were to confront her colleague again, he would only dig in his heels, potentially becoming all the more possessive of Specimen Zero.

"You can't let him win," she told herself, her voice barely audible.

A sudden image of the captive alien flooded her mind: his gentle eyes brimming with sadness, the subtle tremor of his body as he attempted to find even the smallest amount of comfort in his glass beaker. Despite the torment he'd been subjected to, there was an innate kindness in him that somehow transcended the confines of the sterile lab.

"Focus on why you're here," Dr Carver reminded herself.

She turned the tap on and splashed cold water on her face. As the droplets slid down her skin, she imagined them taking away her anger, cleansing her of the negativity that threatened to consume her. She needed a clear head, now more than ever. This was not about her; it was about making sure that Specimen Zero was treated with the care and compassion he deserved.

Slowly, her heart rate began to steady, and her breathing returned to normal. With one last glance at her reflection, she saw the determination etched into her features. Gone was the flustered, angry woman from just minutes before. In her place stood Dr Carver, a scientist with a moral compass that would guide her through even the most challenging of situations.

"Alright," she whispered, drying her hands on a nearby towel. "Let's do this."

Steeling herself for what lay ahead, she pushed open the restroom door and swiftly made her way back to the lab, her eyes instantly drawn to the glass enclosure where Specimen Zero resided. The alien looked up at her, his gaze filled with a mixture of curiosity and dread.

She couldn't help but offer him a smile as she approached the containment area with slow, deliberate steps. Her mind raced, weighing the options available to her. She couldn't confront Dr Fleming again without a plan; she needed to gather concrete evidence that his methods were wrong. And she would have to find a way to protect Specimen Zero in the process.

"Dr Carver."

Dr Fleming's voice cut through her thoughts, jolting her back to the present. She turned to face him, her expression carefully neutral.

"I trust that you've calmed down now," he said plainly. "I know you have your reservations, but we must continue with our work."

"Of course, Dr Fleming," she replied, her voice steady and controlled.

Her eyes locked onto his, and for a moment, she allowed herself to entertain the fantasy of revealing her true intentions. But no; she would bide her time, gather the evidence she needed, and find a way to change the course of this project for the better. For now, she would play the part of the dutiful scientist, all whilst working behind the scenes to ensure Specimen Zero's wellbeing.

Chapter Nineteen

With his weary head propped up by the cold wall of his glass beaker, Ke lay motionless. The dim laboratory lights cast ghostly reflections on the walls, distorting the shadows that surrounded him.

His eyes fluttered beneath closed lids as sleep began to carry him far away from the laboratory's sterile confines. Deep within the crevices of his tortured mind, his subconscious prepared to offer him the warm solace of a place beyond the oppressive walls.

In his dream, an ethereal melody called to him, echoing through the vastness of space. The music felt like an old friend – familiar yet strange. A sound as delicate as drifting snowflakes, he hadn't heard it in a long time. It was the sound of home. As he listened, the melody intertwined with the colours of his memories, painting a vivid picture of the lush valleys, the shimmering rivers, and the crystalline mountains that kissed the sky.

He had grown up in this place, surrounded by nature's beauty, but it had been so long since he'd last seen it with his own eyes. Now, he was there again, enveloped in its tranquillity. He felt a deep longing for the time before life had become so complicated; for when he had been blissfully unaware of the harshness of the world beyond his idyllic home.

"Ke," whispered a voice.

Barely perceptible above the celestial chorus, it was the voice of someone who knew him, the voice of someone who cared for him deeply.

It felt familiar to Ke – like a piece of his past that he'd misplaced in the chaos of his captivity.

"Who are you?" he asked, his tone one of optimism and hope.

"Someone is coming for you," the mysterious figure replied, their form obscured by a swirling mist of stardust. "Hold on for just a little bit longer."

"Are they from my world?" Ke dared to inquire, his chest tightening as both fear and elation coursed through his soul.

"Yes," came the reassuring response, as soft as the wind rustling through the boughs of the ancient trees on his home planet. "You will be free soon."

Ke was overwhelmed by a strange sensation. It grew and slowly filled him until it became a part of him. He felt as though he was walking through the world of his memories again, and yet something about it was different.

He could feel the essence of a newfound strength and courage, like a lion ready to roar. It was the courage to stand up for himself, to fight for what he wanted – a feeling that he had long since forgotten. It was the glow of a warmth that he hadn't felt since he'd been taken from his world. A feeling of peace that seemed to defy the very nature of his reality.

The figure was now silent, but their presence spoke volumes. Somehow, Ke felt certain that this was not just a figment of his imagination, but a true connection to his home, and to those who had not forgotten him.

He took in every detail of the figure: the graceful curves of its robes; the warm, bright colours; the fact that the ethereal music had seemed to be emanating from it. He could feel the stark intensity of each detail with every fibre of his being.

Amidst the silence, Ke felt that the enigmatic figure was giving him the answer to every question that he had ever dared to ask. No longer did even the most difficult of challenges feel impossible.

"Thank you," Ke murmured, tears forming in the corners of his eyes. "Thank you for not giving up on me."

"Never," promised the figure as they began to fade into the cosmic tapestry. "You are never truly alone."

As the majestic saviour vanished into the distance and away into a vapour of nothingness, Ke clung to every detail of the dream: the beauty of the landscape, the love that had radiated from the anonymous voice, and the hope that now coursed through him like a river of liquid light.

He tried to hang on to the notes of the song

until the beautifully sentimental melody lingered in his mind no more. He desperately didn't want to forget the soothing sound of home.

Slowly, the comforting window of hope began to fade and dissolve as reality started to harshly seep back in. With the glass wall of his prison looming before him, and with the chill of the laboratory air penetrating the pores of his delicate skin, Ke blinked away the remnants of his dream. Desperately trying to hold on to the warmth it had provided, he would have given anything to be back in that place of harmonious wonder.

It hurt him to think that it had all just been a dream. It had felt so real, so soothing, so *needed*.

Was it truly just a dream? Did any of it really happen? Could someone be coming to save me from this prison? Please say that it's so!

Although he suspected that nobody outside of the laboratory environment had knowledge of his whereabouts, the dream had awoken something within Ke – a spark of hope that refused to be extinguished. As the lab lights flickered overhead, casting shadows across the room, he made a silent vow to himself that he must *never* lose hope.

Despite his commitment to such hope though, the tears began to fall as he compared the world of his dream to the dire reality of his present surroundings.

Chapter Twenty

As his mind raced back and forth in his confined space, Ke was becoming all the more impatient.

"Dr Fleming!" he called out, desperate to know if his situation would change. "Do you have any updates? Any information at all?"

Dr Fleming was hunched over his computer, furiously typing, and analysing data.

"Patience, Specimen Zero," he said, his voice distant and distracted. "I'm working on it."

Ke tried to still his restless mind, but found it impossible. The anticipation gnawed at him, creating a churning maelstrom of hope and fear that threatened to consume him.

After what felt like an eternity, Dr Fleming

finally looked up from his screen, an unreadable expression on his face.

"Based on my observations so far, I cannot say. Presently, there are still too many variables that need to be addressed."

Ke turned away, unable to look at the scientist any longer. The thought of his people potentially being so near, and yet still so far away, was close to unbearable. He could almost feel the warmth of their presence, the comforting embrace of the family that he'd been torn away from. Despite this, there were no guarantees. He dreaded that the cold, hard reality of his situation was unlikely to change.

As the hours ticked by, Ke found himself drawn to the old English church model once again. Perhaps it was the sense of solace it seemed to offer, or the way it reminded him of the sacred spaces of his own world. He studied the intricate design, tracing the patterns and symbols with a trembling finger, as though trying to absorb some of the peace it represented.

I can't stand it any longer. I must find a way to escape this place.

Chapter Twenty-One

Ke's haunted gaze wandered around the room, longing for the familiar landscapes of his home planet. For days, he had been seriously mulling over his thoughts of escape, and presently, he couldn't shake the feeling that it was now or never. As much as he didn't want to cause harm to Dr Fleming or to anyone else, he knew that he couldn't spend another day in captivity. Certain that the scientists had finished their work for the day, with the lab all to himself for a limited amount of time, he needed to make his move.

This is my chance...

Taking deep breaths to steady himself, he carefully reached behind his back to begin the painstaking process of removing the wires that connected him to several units of machinery. He knew he needed to be fast and quiet; one wrong move could spell disaster.

There would be nothing simple about removing any of the wires. The risk of electrocution and damage to his organs was high, as were the chances of drawing attention to himself should he fail to conceal his inevitable wails of agony. At the very minimum, his back would be dripping with blood.

He knew that following the removal of the first wire, there would be no turning back.

Please let this work...

With trembling fingers, he located the first wire, feeling the smoothness of its cold plastic casing against his sensitive skin. He took a deep breath and steeled himself in anticipation for the pain as he slowly began to twist the wire's connection point back and forth.

Focus. You can do this.

His knuckles white with the strain of holding onto the wire, he tugged cautiously, trying to gauge just how much force he could exert without causing irreparable damage.

A searing jolt of pain shot down his spine as the

wire began to dislodge, the sensation like molten metal tearing through his flesh. As he continued to pull, the pain intensified, each millimetre of progress feeling like an eternity of torment.

A wave of white-hot agony consumed him. But he held on, determined to focus on the freedom that lay just beyond the pain.

Better to risk my life than to live in servitude...

The knowledge of the danger he faced only made his resolve all the more unshakable. He would not allow Dr Fleming to control him anymore.

As the wire loosened and lost contact with Ke's back, a sharp jolt of electricity shot through him, causing his entire body to convulse. He bit down hard on his lower lip, adamant that he mustn't scream. Blood trickled from the bite, but he didn't dare make a sound. Tiny sparks danced around the wire, threatening to escalate into something more dangerous. He couldn't afford to stop now.

As he tried to steady his breathing and slow his racing heart, Ke envisioned the warm embrace of his family, and the soft glow of the twin moons above them. He couldn't forget what he was fighting for.

He moved on to the next wire, his hands slick as he struggled to maintain his grip. Carefully dislodging it, a sudden jolt of electricity raced up his spine. Once again he clenched his jaw to keep from screaming.

For a moment, all he could do was pant, his chest heaving as he fought to regain control of his body and mind. The pain was intense, but the overwhelming relief of having successfully removed the wire was even more powerful.

Some of the wires were entwined with one another, whilst others seemed to be embedded deeper into his flesh than he had initially realised. He refused to be deterred though, even as his energy waned and as his muscles trembled under the strain.

With all but one wire removed, his body felt simultaneously lighter and more battered, as though the very act of freeing himself was taking a toll on his physical form. His vision swam, and he fought to stay conscious as he continued to work, driven by the knowledge that this was plausibly his only chance of escape.

The last wire was the thickest and most deeply embedded of them all, right at the base of his spine. As he twisted and pulled, his vision blurred with tears. It was a struggle to breathe through the searing pain.

Home, family, he thought, the words like a lifeline that anchored him in the midst of his suffering.

And then, with one last pull, and with a guttural cry muffled by his clenched jaw, the wire came loose, leaving a final jagged wound amongst the others in his violently punctured back.

The air around him seemed to lighten, as though the atmosphere itself sensed his triumph. Yet beneath the momentary feeling of elation, Ke knew that the hardest part was still ahead: escaping the confines of the laboratory and returning home. For now though, he had achieved something monumental: he had taken back control of his own body.

Chapter Twenty-Two

Save for the ragged breaths that escaped Ke's lips as he stared down at the now detached wires, the lab was eerily silent. The reality of his situation hit him like a tidal wave: there was no turning back. He glanced nervously at the clock on the wall, its ticking suddenly thunderous in his ears. A human could return at any moment, and should they discover what had transpired, the consequences would be unthinkable.

It was a challenge for Ke to quell the sense of panic that loomed over him.

"Think," he whispered to himself. "I need a plan."

His heart hammered wildly against his chest as he scanned the lab, searching for any means of escape. Although he knew it like the back of his hand, it felt foreign in this moment of desperation. Every cabinet and every instrument seemed to leer at him menacingly, as though they were conspiring with Dr Fleming to keep him trapped.

"Time is running out," he murmured, his voice trembling with terror and urgency. "I need to move fast."

Suddenly, the laboratory door slid open, and in stepped Dr Carver, her brow furrowed in concentration as she set to work on rifling through a stack of papers. The sight of her sent a jolt of alarm through Ke. Instinctively, he recoiled, pressing himself against the farthest end of the cold glass beaker.

As much as he wished to remain unnoticed, it was no use. Almost subconsciously, the scientist caught sight of him, her face a picture of shock.

"Dr Carver!" he blurted out, his voice barely a whisper. "Please, I..."

"Shh," she urged, cutting him off.

Her eyes darted to where the wires had once been connected to him. As her expression shifted from one of surprise to understanding, she quickly crossed the room to speak to the alien quietly through the glass.

"Did you...?"

"Yes," he said breathily, struggling to maintain his composure. "I removed them. I couldn't take it anymore."

"I can't imagine the pain you must have gone through," Dr Carver said softly, looking at him with a mixture of pity and admiration. "That aside though, we need to focus on getting you out of here before Dr Fleming returns."

Ke nodded, his pulse quickening as he realised that his goal of escape was no longer a solitary endeavour. Suddenly, there was hope – a glimmer of light in the darkness that had consumed him for so long. He allowed himself a small, tentative smile.

"Thank you," he whispered, the gratitude evident in his eyes.

Dr Carver stole a furtive glance at the laboratory door. She could only pray that Dr Fleming wouldn't appear. Her trembling fingers reached for the cabinet, the cool metal handle sending chills up her spine. The key to the lock on Specimen Zero's glass beaker lay inside, and tonight, she would set him free.

"Dr Carver," Ke whispered, his voice soft and humble. "I... I can't thank you enough."

"Save your thanks until we're out of here," she replied, forcing a grin she didn't feel.

She knew the risk she was taking by betraying her colleague, but every fibre of her being told her that it was the right thing to do.

As she retrieved the key, Ke watched her with wide eyes – a blend of awe and disbelief swirling within. His energy seemed to radiate from the glass beaker, filling the room with an ethereal warmth. He couldn't believe what was happening. It terrified him to think that perhaps he was merely having a dream that could shatter at any moment.

"Is this really happening?" he murmured.

His vulnerability tore at Dr Carver's emotions, igniting a fierce protectiveness within her. She clenched the key tightly in her palm, determined to see her plan through.

"Trust me," she said, her voice barely audible but resolute. "I'll get you out of here."

In the instant that Ke met her gaze, she felt a connection deeper than anything that she'd ever experienced before. A bond forged through shared hope and desperation. In the alien's eyes, she saw the kindness that had been stifled for far too long – ironically the very spiritual essence that Dr Fleming sought to exploit.

With a trembling hand, Dr Carver inserted the cold metal key into the padlock that secured Specimen Zero's beaker. The temperature in the room seemed to plummet as she twisted it, her breath catching when the key refused to yield.

"*Come on*," she muttered under her breath, forcing herself to remain calm as she tried again. "Please work."

"What's wrong?" Ke asked, concern lacing his sweet voice.

He leaned closer into the beaker's glass, his eyes searching the woman's for reassurance. She gritted her teeth, frustration bubbling within her like molten lava.

"Dr Fleming must have swapped the key," she said, her voice gravelly with anger. "He doesn't trust me."

"Are you sure?"

"Undoubtedly," she said. "He has always been paranoid about keeping you contained."

"No!" said Ke, struggling to keep his voice low as the uncertainty of his situation weighed heavily upon him.

"Let me think," Dr Carver said, her mind racing. "We might not have much time before Dr Fleming returns. We need to find another way to get you out."

Darting frantically around the lab in search of an alternative, the woman's eyes quickly locked onto a metal stool in the corner. She knew what had to be done.

"Stand back, and prepare yourself," she instructed.

Her breath hitched as she gripped the cold metal stool with all her strength. She held it aloft, ready to strike at full force. As the alien pressed his bloodstained body against the far side of his enclosure, his trust in her unwavering, it ignited a spark of courage within her. With a tightened grip on the stool, she sharply exhaled and swung it at the glass beaker in one charged swoop.

The sound of shattering glass shimmered loudly throughout the laboratory, shards flying in every direction like a storm of razor-sharp rain. As the cacophony subsided, Dr Carver blinked away tears and lowered her arms, staring at the remains of the alien's prison.

"Quick!" she whispered urgently. "You need to get out of here before Dr Fleming can even sense anything."

Ke hesitated for a brief moment, the enormity of his newfound freedom washing over him. Then, with a grace that defied his shock and bewilderment, he jumped down from the shattered remnants of his beaker and landed elegantly on the lab floor, the shards of glass no match for his hardened soles. The sensation of the cold tiles beneath his feet was foreign and exhilarating.

"Thank you, Dr Carver," he murmured, inclining his head in gratitude.

Dr Carver could see the emotions emanating from the innocent alien – relief, fear, and humility.

"Let's not celebrate just yet," she cautioned, her gaze flickering to the door. "You're still not safe."

Chapter Twenty-Three

Ke's pulse thumped against his chest, a rhythm that matched the sheer feeling of panic in his gut. The sterile scent of disinfectant filled his nostrils as he tried to focus on his next move.

"If you don't get out of here now, you could be a prisoner forever," said Dr Carver, her resolve unwavering.

Suddenly, the laboratory door slid open, revealing the stern figure of Dr Fleming. His eyes glinted with malevolence, and a twisted smile played upon his lips as he approached them.

"Ah, Specimen Zero," he cooed. "I see that you've been conspiring against me."

Dr Fleming's efforts to appear calm were futile.

The vein on his forehead throbbed on his furiously red face as he began to walk towards the alien in a calculating manner.

"Stay away from him!" Dr Carver shouted, positioning herself between her colleague and the alien.

"Or what?" Dr Fleming snapped. "You'll defy me too? Your loyalty to Specimen Zero is touching, Dr Carver, but all the same, it is misplaced. You have no idea what you're getting yourself into."

"Neither do you," Ke retorted.

Shocked by his own words, the alien's whole body surged with horror and rebellion. Throughout the entirety of his captivity, he had never spoken to Dr Fleming with such defiance.

"Is that a threat?" Dr Fleming challenged, stepping closer. "Do you really think you can escape?"

"Let me go," Ke demanded, his voice trembling. "Do the right thing. Choose a different path."

"Pathetic," Dr Fleming mocked. "Foolish."

Ke didn't want to hurt his captor, but as the angry man advanced even closer towards him, there was no other option.

"Enough!" Ke cried out.

Defensively extending his arm out in one swift movement, he released a surge of energy that sent Dr Fleming reeling backwards. As the man crashed into a shelf of delicate equipment, the sound of shattering glass once again echoed throughout the soulless laboratory.

Ke stood there shaking, the full extent of his actions beginning to sink in.

"Goodbye, Dr Fleming," he declared, his eyes blazing with resistance. "I've asked you nicely for my freedom. I've even begged – many times over. I can't stay here anymore. I've reached my limit. You can't keep me here."

Unwilling to accept defeat, Dr Fleming scrambled around on the floor, ready to get back up and fight.

"Run!" Dr Carver urged, grabbing the alien's arm. "We've got to get you out of here before security turns up!"

As they sprinted towards the door, the lab now in chaos behind them, Ke couldn't help but wonder what consequences his actions might bring. Would this be the beginning of his salvation, or the catalyst for his ultimate destruction?

Chapter Twenty-Four

The blaring alarm pierced the air, its shrill cry punctuating the frenzy that had erupted. The walls seemed to close in around Ke as he and Dr Carver sprinted down a poorly lit corridor, the laboratory's pungent smell of disinfectant still lingering.

"Where are we going?" he asked, panting.

"An exit – any exit!" Dr Carver replied, her eyes darting from wall to wall. "Dr Fleming will have security on us soon."

Ke's head swirled with conflicting thoughts, his earlier actions playing over and over in his mind. He had harmed another being – something that he'd sworn never to do. And yet, he couldn't shake the feeling that perhaps it had been necessary; that maybe, just maybe, it had been the only way to save himself. Also, now that he had demonstrated the physical strength of his kind, perhaps the domineering scientist would think twice about wanting to keep another extraterrestrial captive.

"Left!" Dr Carver shouted.

They careened around a corner, accidentally knocking over a trolley of surgical instruments that sent a haunting metallic clatter echoing down the hall.

Ke could only breathe in shallow gasps as they continued.

"There's an emergency exit up ahead," Dr Carver said between strained breaths. "We just have to make it before anyone can catch us."

As they rounded another bend, they could hear the sound of distant footsteps. The threatening noise grew louder, gaining on them with every passing second.

"Dr Carver," Ke implored, fear settling like ice in his veins. "What if we don't make it? What will happen to you?"

"Don't worry about me," she said, her voice firm despite the terror that flickered in her eyes. "I'll fight for you."

"Even if it means causing more harm?" Ke asked, his own moral dilemma threatening to throw him off course.

"Sometimes we must choose the lesser of two evils," Dr Carver replied, her eyes never leaving the path ahead. "Now come on. We're almost there."

The air seemed to crackle with tension as they raced forward, freedom hanging in the balance. The echoing footsteps were nearly upon them now, their pursuers only moments behind.

And then, just as the door marked 'EMERGENCY EXIT' in bold red letters was in sight, the unthinkable happened: a gunshot rang out, its deafening crackle reverberating through the hallway.

"Go!" Dr Carver screamed, shoving Ke towards the exit, her face contorted with pain. "Save yourself!"

"Dr Carver!" Ke cried out.

He was torn between his need to escape and his

loyalty to the woman who had risked everything to help him. Caught in the grip of indecision, he hesitated as the sound of heavy boots drew ever closer.

Chapter Twenty-Five

With a sudden burst of determination, Ke turned back to Dr Carver, his mind made up.

"I won't leave you!" he shouted, running towards her prone figure.

Another gunshot rang out, the bullet whizzing past the high peak of Ke's head as he reached the woman and lifted her into his arms. With a grunt of effort, he carried her towards the door, panic thumping in his chest like a caged beast.

The footsteps grew louder still, the sound of angry voices filling the air as the guards closed in.

Ke refused to give up, his mind focused solely on the goal of escape. He reached the door and kicked it open, the blinding light of day momentarily disorientating him. Having lived only under artificial lighting for so long, the sun seemed almost cruel.

He burst through the doorway and into the unknown beyond. As he fled into the glare of the great outdoors, he stumbled and nearly fell. Blinking rapidly to adjust to his drastic change of environment, he looked around at his surroundings, his features contorting in disbelief. His breath hitched in his throat as the dry, hot air invaded his lungs. It was in stark contrast to the timeless, climate-controlled laboratory that he had grown so used to.

The research facility, it seemed, was in the middle of nowhere. All around him stretched an endless expanse of barren desert, the air shimmering with waves of heat across the landscape. With no signs of civilisation, there was nothing but sand dunes and scraggly shrubs as far as the eye could see.

Ke realised with a sinking feeling that the laboratory's location was intentional. Hidden away in the middle of the desert to keep its true purpose a secret, no one would stumble upon it by accident. It was the perfect site for anyone wishing to hold another being captive against their will.

A raging fury began to burn within Ke. It mingled potently with the fear and confusion that still gripped him. How could any human be so cruel and so unfeeling as to subject another soul to such torment? It was sickening.

A myriad of thoughts rushed through his mind, and although his adjustment to the outside world had taken mere seconds, Ke frantically shook his head, desperate to refocus. There was no time to lose.

He took a clumsy step forward, the sand shifting beneath his feet. As he stumbled again, his legs weak from exertion, he fell down. Never did he release Dr Carver from his grip though. Still holding her in his arms, he quickly got back up and started to run. He knew that he needed to get further away from the research facility in order to properly assess the woman's condition.

As his feet pounded against the sand, he could only hope that the young scientist would be ok.

He sprinted through the scorching desert, his clawed feet kicking up a trail of dust behind him. The blazing sun beat down on his peridot skin, but the heat was nothing compared to the terror that fuelled him. His breath came in gasps, his chest heaving with effort as he glanced nervously down at Dr Carver. As she lay limp in the cradle of his arms, her once-vibrant eyes were now glazed over and unresponsive. A deep red stain spread across her white lab coat. It appeared to be coming from the bullet wound that had struck her down as they'd fled.

"Dr Carver," Ke whispered, his voice choked with emotion. "Stay with me. *You have to stay with me.*"

With every step, he could feel the weight of their pursuers closing in, their menacing shouts echoing through the arid landscape. He had no choice but to keep running. As much as he wanted to check on the woman in his arms, nothing could be done until they were a safe distance away from their enemies.

"Please, Dr Carver," he begged frantically, desperation clinging to every syllable. "Hold on."

Finally, after what felt like hours of running, they reached a formation of large rocks. Satisfied that it would provide adequate cover from both the sun's relentless glare and from any prying eyes, with great care, Ke laid Dr

Carver down in its shade. Highly aware that the woman's body was unnervingly silent, tears streamed down his face as he said a quiet prayer.

Despair gnawed at him as he hesitated for a moment, trying to gather the courage to examine her injuries.

"Amelia?" he said softly, searching her face for any signs of life.

He took a deep breath, and after respectfully removing the layers of covering clothing, began to inspect the gunshot wound. A lump rose in his throat as he realised the extent of the damage. The bullet had pierced her lung, and she had lost a lot of blood.

"Dr Carver… I'm so sorry," he murmured, his voice cracking with regret.

Consumed by a stark, unbearable grief, he looked up to the sky and screamed, the pain tearing through him in a frenzy of anguish. How could this have happened? She had only wanted to help him, and now she was gone.

As he wept over her lifeless body, Ke vowed to himself that he wouldn't let Dr Carver's death be in vain. He would carry the memory of her with him as he continued on his journey, honouring her kindness and bravery. Not only would he do everything in his power to find a way back home; he would repay the debt he owed her – by putting an end to Dr Fleming's unethical approach to research once and for all.

Chapter Twenty-Six

The desert wind howled like a mournful spirit, kicking up clouds of dust that stung Ke's face. He stood over Dr Carver's lifeless body, his heart heavy with sorrow and guilt. The sun bore down on them, relentless and unforgiving. He couldn't leave her exposed like this. She deserved better.

"Forgive me, Dr Carver," he whispered, wiping the sweat from his brow as he bent down to lift her gently in his arms. "I will do everything I can to give you the send-off you deserve."

With a purposeful gaze, he surveyed the desolate landscape around him, searching for an appropriate spot to lay her to rest.

"Over there," he muttered, nodding at a small cluster of rocks.

As he carried her over, he couldn't help but recall the warmth of her smile, and the way that she'd gone above and beyond to help him escape from Dr Fleming's unyielding captivity. And now, all he could feel was the cold weight of her body in his arms.

"Please, may your soul find peace," he said.

He laid her down on the sand. With tears blurring his vision as he began to dig, his clawed hands scraped through the dry dust beneath him. He knew it would take hours to create a proper grave, but every handful of sand felt like a step towards absolution.

"I'm so sorry I couldn't save you," he said quietly, pausing in his labour to wipe away the tears that streamed down his face. "But I promise you this: I will carry the memory of you with me always, and I will find a way to make sure that no other being has to suffer at the hands of Dr Fleming."

As the hours wore on, the sun dipped lower in the sky, casting long shadows across the desert. The once-blistering heat gave way to a biting chill, but Ke pressed on, driven by both his grief and his determination.

"Let this be a testament to your goodness, Dr Carver," he declared as the grave grew deeper, his voice barely audible over the wind's sorrowful wail. "Your compassion will not be forgotten."

Finally, as the stars began to appear in the darkening sky, Ke knew it was time. He lowered the sweet woman's body into the ground, whispering words of gratitude and farewell as he gently covered her with sand.

"May you find peace within the eternal galaxy, my friend," he whispered, his voice hoarse with emotion. "And may your spirit guide me on this journey."

After one last look at the simple grave, Ke turned away. He was on a mission now; not only to return home, but to ensure that Dr Amelia Carver's legacy would live on. As he set off into the night, fuelled by thoughts of the woman who had shown him kindness even in the face of the most unimaginable darkness, he felt a newfound sense of purpose guiding him forward.